THE TEARDROP BABY

The TEARDROP BABY

by KAREN RADLER GREENFIELD
pictures by SHARLEEN COLLICOTT

A Laura Geringer Book
An Imprint of HarperCollinsPublishers

The Teardrop Baby
Text copyright © 1994 by Karen Radler Greenfield
Illustrations copyright © 1994 by Sharleen Collicott
Printed in the U.S.A. All rights reserved.

Library of Congress Cataloging-in-Publication Data
Greenfield, Karen.
    The teardrop baby / by Karen Radler Greenfield ; pictures by Sharleen Collicott.
        p.   cm.
    "A Laura Geringer book."
    Summary: After longing for years for a baby, a couple is given one made from their teardrops by a wizard woman, but after seven years, she takes him away from them.
    ISBN 0-06-022943-8. — ISBN 0-06-022944-6 (lib. bdg.)
    [1. Babies—Fiction.   2. Magic—Fiction.   3. Crying—Fiction.]   I. Collicott, Sharleen, ill.   II. Title.
PZ7.G8453Te   1994   93-29603
[E]—dc20   CIP
                                                                                                             AC

Typography by Christine Kettner
1   2   3   4   5   6   7   8   9   10
❖
First Edition

For my children, Caitlin and Nicholas
—K. R. G.

These pictures are dedicated to my son Eric,
who has been to the edge of the world and home—
several times.
—S. C.

NCE THERE WAS
A MAN AND A WOMAN who cried all the time because they had everything they wanted except a child of their own.

The man and woman carried buckets on their shoulders and collected their tears to make their garden grow. "If only we had a child of our own, we would be truly happy," they cried, sloshing tears over roses, pansies, carnations, and snapdragons.

One day a ragged wizard woman shuffled by, carrying a loaf of bread. It was the middle of winter. Everything was covered with snow.

"I've never seen roses growing in snow," said the ragged wizard woman. "What's your secret?" The man and woman heaved a bucketful of tears onto the frosty rose bed, and baby buds unfolded.

"Put down those buckets," said the ragged wizard woman, "and tell me what this is all about."

"Ragged wizard woman," sobbed the man and woman, "we want a child of our own."

"Save your tears for tonight," said the ragged wizard woman. "And meet me here in the garden. Remember," she warned, "tonight a baby will be yours. But his future is mine. I'll be back." Then she bopped the man and woman with her magic baguette. Stars collided in the afternoon sky. And the ragged wizard woman vanished from sight.

That night, when the moon rose full, the man and woman met the ragged wizard woman in the garden. Instead of buckets they carried a cradle. "Put down the cradle," said the ragged wizard woman. "When I'm gone, look inside. You'll find your baby. But remember . . ." Then she walked around the cradle three times, grunting:

"Mama-tu-mama
Mama-tu-mama
Mama-tu-mama"

The ragged wizard woman shuffled away muttering an old lullaby.

"Mama Sweetbreath and
All her children
Rock in a chair
The size of an ocean.
She watches them come,
She watches them grow,
She feeds them on turnips
And rolls them in snow.

She gives them a song,
A dance and a star,
A spoon and a cup
And sends them afar.
Her baby is dreaming
The world is divine.
Tonight, Mama Sweetbreath,
The baby is mine."

When the man and the woman could no longer hear the ragged wizard woman's song, they peeked into the cradle. "Where is the baby?" they wailed. "We've been tricked!" Then they began to cry into the cradle until the cradle was full of tears.

Suddenly the man and woman stopped. The moon sparkled high overhead. "What's that?" they gasped, seeing the reflection of a baby in the cradle full of tears. They reached in, but the baby just slipped through their fingers. "Teardrops," they sobbed and hid their faces from the freezing air.

Then they looked again. The teardrops had turned to ice. "It *is* a baby," they marveled, reaching

into the cradle. And they held the baby of ice while they sang the ragged wizard woman's lullaby.

As they sang, the ice cracked. The baby melted away.

Soon, all that was left was a shimmering sliver of a baby—just a reflection that looked something like the man, something like the woman, as if the reflection of the man and woman had gotten mixed up together in the cradle of tears.

And then, suddenly, the man and woman remembered.

"Mama-tu-mama."

"Mama-tu-mama," they grunted, circling the cradle. *"Mama-tu-mama,"* they shouted. The moon slipped behind a cloud. *"Mama-tu-mama."* Lightning streaked. *"Mama-tu-mama."* The baby of ice disappeared. In their arms, the man and woman held a child of their own.

Perhaps the man and woman should have been completely happy now, but, as you can see, they were not. For a day and a night they feared the ragged wizard woman would come back for the baby. "When," wondered the man and woman, "does today become the future?"

The sun rose the second day, and the man and woman had barely slept.

Just before noon, again the ragged wizard woman came shuffling by with her magic baguette. "I forgot to tell you something," she said. "I live on the edge of the world, far from here. But that's not all." Then she fell asleep on her elbows, one eye open, keeping watch on the baby.

While she slept, the woman cooed and kissed her baby. The man was busy heaping treasures to offer in trade for the baby's future.

Moments before sunset, the ragged wizard woman awoke. She grabbed her baguette. "Ah, my magic loaf!" she said. And she tore off a piece with a flourish. "Your baby's fortune is here in this loaf."

Then she read from a slip of paper she pulled
from the baguette:

*"Baked in the bread, the future is told. The boy will be
mine when he's seven years old.*

"Offer me nothing," she told the man and woman. "His future is with me!"

Then the ragged wizard woman spun around and shuffled away, tossing bread crumbs behind her.

For seven years, the man and woman did enjoy their teardrop boy. Every morning, the woman would rock her baby in her arms, singing rhyming words, while the man served him pancakes with honey butter.

Every afternoon, the man would run with the boy through the meadows, then home again in time for supper.

Together, in the evening, they would tell stories of piglets and bunnies and a little gray mouse who befriended a swan.

After a while, the man and woman lost track of the passage of time. "Today cannot be the future," they would say to each other. "Today the child is still ours." But seven years finally came to an end, and one moonless night the ragged wizard woman returned.

"Your baby is dreaming the world is divine," the ragged wizard woman whispered as the man and woman slept unawares. "Tonight, Mama Sweetbreath, the baby is mine."

And the teardrop boy awoke to find himself alone with the ragged wizard woman at the edge of the world.

Rock and sand stretched out ahead as if the edge were not a place with a beginning and an end. No flowers or trees grew at the edge of the world.

The boy could hear no birds singing. He could see no shadows or shade. Just an old clay oven stood nearby. Startled to find himself there, the boy wondered why he had never heard of the ragged wizard woman before.

"You are mine now," the ragged wizard woman

said to the child. "And now you will be my bread boy. Take these buckets, bread boy. Fill them with sand. Be back before the end of the day. We have work to do."

"I don't much care for her," the child said to himself when she had gone. "Her home is not nice. She smells like mold. If only I had my mother and father."

Then the teardrop boy, who had never cried a tear in his life, began to cry into the buckets.

"What's this?" the child gasped, sloshing tears over rock and sand. Toadflax, blanketflowers, yarrow, and bluebells sprang up around him. His tears ran in rivulets before him, and a path bloomed—mountain garland, lupines, cornflowers, and lemon mint.

Quickly gathering the wildflowers, the boy went to look for a place to hide them.

Far behind the oven, hidden from view, the boy found a bit of sand surrounded by jagged rock. There he tucked the flowers under a few pebbles.

Then he surprised himself and cried again, and, again, wildflowers bloomed around him as his tears fell. Soon the edge of the world began to look a

little more like home. Fearing the ragged wizard
woman would return any moment, the boy ran to
fill his buckets with sand.

When the ragged wizard woman returned she began to make her bread and bake in the fortunes she kept in the pocket of her dress.

She taught the boy how to bake bread. She showed him how to mix the batter, adding a bucket of sand for every loaf. Then she stirred in a fortune just before baking. When the bread was done, the ragged wizard woman would sing.

"Winter wheat, summer wheat,
Rye, barley, bran,
Millet and corn
And a bucket of sand.
Put in the fortune
And watch the bread rise. . . .
Who will be rich?
Who will be wise?
Into the oven,
The moon's overhead.
The future is cast
And baked in the bread."

The ragged wizard woman kept the boy busy. The boy was as brave as could be and worked very hard every day. He swept the sand, filled the buckets, oiled the squeak in the oven door. He helped make the bread and watched the ragged wizard woman very, very carefully.

Whenever she was gone, the boy would return to his secret rock, and all alone, he would think of his mother and father and cry his secret tears, and the ragged wizard woman never knew that day by day, the edge of the world was coming closer and closer to home. Bluebells, primrose, poppy flowers, Queen Anne's lace, black-eyed Susans sprang up here and there as the boy's tears ran on and on through the sand around the rock-strewn desert, right across the edge.

One day, the ragged wizard woman left the boy, saying, "Tonight is the first full moon in spring. I will be gone until morning. Bake a loaf of bread for breakfast and fill an extra bucket of sand. Tomorrow we will bake all day."

That night, when the moon rose full, the boy baked the breakfast loaf. He mixed the batter, added the sand, and almost put the bread in the oven before he remembered . . .

Midnight stars danced merrily as the teardrop boy sang the ragged wizard woman's song.

The next morning, the ragged wizard woman asked for her loaf.

"I forgot to tell you something," said the boy.

"Wait 'til I've finished," she said with a flourish as she tore off a piece of the bread. "Oh, no!" she gasped. "I've been tricked!" Then she read the fortune the boy had baked into the bread:

TODAY, RAGGED WIZARD WOMAN,
THE FUTURE IS MY OWN!

"Do you know what this means?" she shrieked. "What have you done to my breakfast bun? And what have you done to me?"

Then the teardrop boy, knowing he would soon
be home where he belonged, cried a river of joyful

tears, which carried him over the edge of the world, into his mother's arms.

After that, the teardrop boy and the man and woman were as happy as could be. All around the house in neat little rows were asters and tulips and marigolds and petunias. But behind, as far as anyone could see, wildflowers grew, beyond the edge of the sky.

And every year, for the next six years, when the moon was full in winter, the man and woman cried a cradle full of tears.

After that, as you can see, they were very, very busy.

As for the ragged wizard woman, she was never heard from again.

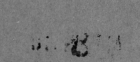